Daddy's Dare

Best Friend's Dad Romance

Kaci Rose

Five Little Roses Publishing

Copyright

Book Cover By: **Sarah Kil Creative Studio**
Cover Girl Design
Editing By: Debbe @ **On The Page, Author and PA Services**
Proofread By: Ashley @ **Geeky Girl Author Services**
Violet Rae

Blurb

She's the one person he can't have. The one person he wants. His daughter's best friend.

Club Red was my safe haven. The one place I could go and let go of everything.
Then she walked in.
My daughter's best friend.
No way was I letting anyone else play with her, show her around, or touch her.
I dared her to give me one night.
One dare turns into two, spend the day at the pool with me.
Dare 3? Forever...
Only we won't be getting our happily ever after, but I will make sure she does.

A Best Friend's Father, Age Gap, Summer Romance

Welcome to a filthy dirty summer! Drop it like it's hot with your 17 favorite instalove authors! Each stand-alone story delivers a scorching, fantasy-fueled romance! No need to pack a swimsuit—your kindle is all you need for a wet and wild summer!

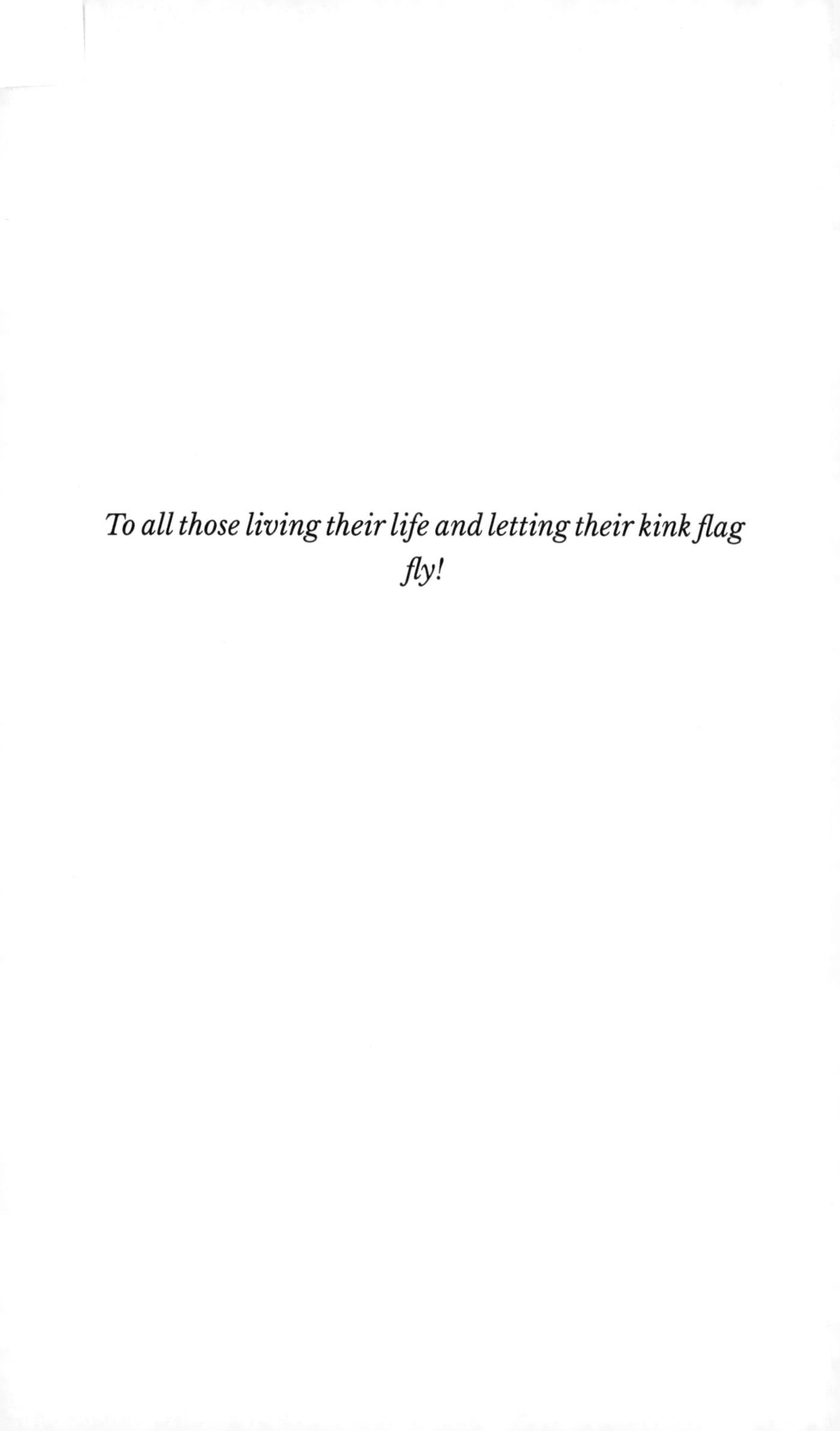

To all those living their life and letting their kink flag fly!

Contents

Get Free Books!

Do you like Military Men? Best friends brothers?
What about sweet, sexy, and addicting books?

If you join Kaci Rose's Newsletter you get these books free!

https://www.kacirose.com/free-books/
Now on to the story!

Chapter 1

Summer

I don't get out much. My roommate's solution? Dragging me out to Club Red, a sex club. We read many of the same books, which in her head translates to me loving this club as she does.

But I have to admit I am interested. I mean, how can I not be? After all, I read about these things in my books, yet to go to one in person? A completely different ball game.

This is so far outside my comfort zone that I can't even *see* my comfort zone from here. But I must admit that the whole club's idea excites me. Which is why I let her dress me up in this skintight black dress I swear is no more than a slip from under another dress.

It barely covers my ass, and it makes my breasts pop. I can't wear a bra, but it's supposed to have a built-in one, which is nothing more than an extra layer of fabric. She promises I can wear her long sweater over it, which will only make me stick out even more in the hot Chicago summer.

As we stand outside the door of what looks like a warehouse, I second guess myself. I trust Skye, and we were friends for years before becoming roommates, but we're different people. I have so many "what ifs" floating around in my head. What if I want to leave and can't find her? What if I hate it?

"Take a deep breath," Skye says. "You can leave at any time. Here are my car keys, so if you want to leave early, I'll catch a ride. I know plenty of people here."

Skye has always been good at reading my mind, especially when it starts to spin out of control. It's why we fit even though we're so different.

Taking another deep breath, I take the keys from her and step through the glass door you can't see from the street. I have no idea what I expected, but the clean, bright lobby we step into isn't it. It looks like any other lobby in any other waiting room across the country. You would never know that on the other side of the big leather double doors sits one of Chicago's most notorious BDSM clubs.

Skye knows the receptionist, but I don't hear much while they chat. Skye takes the paperwork from my hand she had me fill out before we came. She's sponsoring me for a thirty-day guest membership, which means we had to get a doctor's physical, an STD test, proof I'm on birth control and fill out a series of consent and liability forms.

I look over the rules form. Don't interrupt other people's scenes. Stop doesn't mean stop; red means stop. There are plain-clothed monitors everywhere and marked security. Paragraphs detail what to do if a scene goes wrong. The consequences for breaking the rules and everything in between are clearly stated.

As weird as it sounds, the paperwork makes me feel calmer about the whole situation. The lady at the desk takes my ID and photo and, a few minutes later, hands me my discreet membership card. It's a deep red with the word "membership" at the top and a member number. On the back is a barcode with no mention of the club, nor is my name included.

"All right, let me give you the grand tour," Skye says. "You can find the restrooms and locker rooms through that door, but you can also get there from the main floor. The club office is down this hall."

I follow her while she puts our stuff in her locker and shows me the code, the same one on our alarm at home.

"But now on to the main event," Skye continues as we walk back into the lobby and up to the big double doors at the end.

The security guys on either side open them for us, but neither speaks. Instead, they nod hello to Skye.

I'm not prepared for the room we step into. It has an old warehouse feel with the black cement floors in the wide-open space.

"There's a two-drink maximum, but you can get all the water you need, and they have finger food snacks at the bar." Skye points to our right at the massive bar with at least twenty barstools sitting around it.

In front of us is the largest sectional couch I've ever seen. It can easily hold twenty people. Large ottomans are scattered between the sectional and the bar, big enough to hold five people lying down—more if everyone is sitting up.

The seating area is decorated in black leather with red accents. The lights are low, and as my eyes adjust, I see a stage beyond the sitting area where people are performing.

"The archway to the left of the bar leads to the voyeur hall, where all sorts of different themed rooms are located. If the curtains are open, you're free to watch. The second floor has more themed and private rooms. Again, if the curtains are open, you can watch. But there's also a more intimate lounge setting, which you can see from below." Skye points up to the row of glass above us.

It's almost like a hotel lobby where you look up and see the row of rooms, except there's no hallway, only walls of glass up to three stories.

"What's on the third floor?" I ask, staring up at the glass walls.

"Those are the VIP suites. They're the ones who pay every month to have a private suite. You can't get there unless you're invited, so only worry about the first and second floors. Now let's get you a drink because trust me, you'll need one."

Skye tucks a strand of long curly hair behind her ear and steers me toward the bar, where she orders us a drink.

Now my eyes have adjusted, I turn and stare at the huge space again. Couples are scattered everywhere, many without clothes. On one of the ottomans, a man has a woman held down with one hand and is playing with her under her skirt with the other. The sight turns me on. It's like watching a live porno, but much sexier.

"I see you found something you like. You can watch anyone out here. You can join in only if they ask, but they won't be offended if you don't. Text me before you leave. I'm going to go meet a friend." Skye grins and heads off toward the stage at the back of the room.

I scan the room again, and a woman on the couch catches my eye. She offers me a smile as her man is on his knees with his head between her thighs. The sight makes me hot, and it's right in the open. Trying to get relief from the tingling in my core, I sit on one of the bar stools.

"Summer?"

I look over to see my best friend, Gemma's dad. "Knox?" I ask in shock.

Of all the people to run into my first time here. To have to explain this to him. So much for not having to tell anyone about tonight.

"What are you doing here?" He looks as shocked as me.

"My roommate thought I needed to get out, and she's a regular, so here I am." I give him the shortened version.

This is Gemma's dad, who also happens to be the man I've been crushing on for longer than I want to admit. I've been infatuated with him for as long as I can remember, and seeing him here gives me mixed feelings. Is this why Gemma and I never saw him date? Because he was here instead?

He sits on the barstool next to me and looks me over, his eyes landing on the glass in my hand. "How many drinks have you had?"

"Just the one." I hold up my half-finished drink.

Taking the glass from me, he orders water and hands it to me, falling right back into the caretaker role. I've been best friends with his daughter for years, and he's always taken care of me when I've been at his house. I feel bad he thinks he has to do that here in what should be his safe space. But not bad enough to get up and leave because I feel safe with him next to me.

He sips from his drink for a few minutes, and behind his eyes, I see the same war waging inside me. Walk away like we should or keep talking to see where it goes. When I sip my water, he speaks again.

"See anything you like?" He points to the room.

His words shock me, and I fall silent. He smirks and waits for me to answer.

Stalling, I look out over the crowd again, and for a moment, I don't see anybody. I'm trying to wrap my head around my best friend's dad sitting next to me, asking if I like any of the sex scenes playing out in front of me.

I nod to the couple I saw earlier where he's still holding her down on the ottoman.

Knox's eyes follow mine, and he nods in approval. "What about them?" He nods to a couple on the other side of the ottoman.

The man has a woman tied to a Saint Andrews cross and is roughly having his way with her. My body heats watching them. I turn back to find Knox looking at me. Once I turned eighteen, he insisted I call him Knox since we were both adults. It shifted our relationship slightly as if he now sees more of an equal. Of course, it could all be in my head.

"I dare you to forget the walls between us and let me help you experience the club for one night."

Damn, this man knows I would never turn down a dare.

Chapter 2

Knox

I can't believe Summer is sitting on the barstool next to me. Much less that she's here in Club Red. My daughter's best friend, who ever since she turned eighteen, I've had the most inappropriate thoughts about. The girl who once she turned eighteen has made it impossible for me to connect even casually with any other woman.

Even though I come to the club and try not to think about her, it's never worked. I thought I was hallucinating when I saw her sitting at the bar. I was sure it had to be someone who resembled her, but the closer I got, the more it looked like Summer.

I can't believe I dared her. This girl hasn't turned down a dare, not once in all the years she's been friends with my daughter. She would be well within her rights to make this the first one she turns down, but I hold my breath and say a silent prayer she doesn't.

She looks around one more time before taking a deep breath and nodding. "Okay. One night."

My dick, which was already hard seeing her in this sexy skintight dress, gets even harder. "Can I touch you?"

Club Red is all about permission and consent. You can't touch anyone without their permission, or they'll revoke your membership and ban you from the grounds.

"Yes."

"Do you remember your safe words?" I need to be sure because I don't want to push her past her limits. I certainly don't want to give her a reason to regret even a moment of tonight.

"Green if I'm good to go, yellow if I'm reaching a limit, and red to stop everything." She recites what I'm sure they told her when she walked in this evening.

Good enough.

I take her hand in mine and help her off the bar stool, leading her to the empty end of the large couch. Sitting down with plenty of room between me and the other couple, I grip her waist and pull her onto my lap so her back is to my chest. I move my hands down her sides, hooking them under her knees and putting one on either side of my legs, spreading her wide.

She immediately tries to close her legs, like I thought she would.

"No, no. Keep them open unless you want to use a safe word. Do you want to use a safe word?"

"No," she whispers.

When I spread my legs wider, I force her to dress up her thighs. If she isn't wearing underwear, anyone who looks at her will be able to tell.

"Are you wearing underwear?" I murmur in her ear as I lightly trail one hand up her thigh, intent on finding out.

"Yes," she whispers again.

When she wiggles on my lap, I wrap one arm around her waist to hold her in place as I trail my other hand under her dress, coming in contact with the lace keeping us separated.

She's soaked, and it makes my cock twitch. I'm sure she feels it digging into her ass, but I ignore it. This is for her.

"Look at the way he's holding her down. She's pinned and unable to move as he takes her. Is that what you like?" I ask, redirecting her attention to the couple she noticed earlier.

I lightly run my fingers over the soaked lace of her panties. Her breathing increases and her nipples are hard peaks under her dress, all signs she loves what she sees.

"What do you like better? That he's holding her down, or that he's taking what he wants from her?" I coax, wanting to understand her more.

I shouldn't want to. Hell, I shouldn't be touching her. I should be sending her on her way with the promise not to bring this up to Gemma, who doesn't know this side of me.

Hell, if I can walk away now. If I'm going to crash and burn, it will be tonight with the memory of her here.

"Him taking," she breathes.

Though she's shy, that's okay. I can work with shyness. I love that about her.

"Keep watching then, Princess. Watch him take what he wants from her and her loving every minute of it."

She obeys and keeps her eyes on the couple as I move the soaked lace to the side and run my fingers through her folds. She gasps but doesn't stop me. Her juices coat my fingers before I bring them to her clit and start gently playing with it.

"What about the couple at the other end of the sectional?" I redirect her attention to a man sitting on the couch where a woman kneels as he slams his cock in and out of her mouth. She's given control to him in the ultimate sign of trust.

"I... I don't know," she says as she watches them. Her body doesn't respond as much as the first couple, so I tuck the knowledge into the back of my head.

"What about the St. Andrews Cross?" I nod behind the seating area, and when her eyes land on the woman restrained there, I swear she gushes on my hand.

I have my answer, but she still shakes her head.

"Keep your eyes on them," I tell her as I kiss her neck and thrust two fingers into her.

She moans, drawing the eyes of a few people around us, but her eyes are on the woman being taken roughly. Only it's not by the same man as earlier. That man is standing to the side, playing with her breasts.

I move the hand gripping her waist up to her gorgeous perky breasts and start playing with them in much the same way the man is playing with the woman Summer is watching.

When I pick up the pace with my fingers thrusting inside her and my thumb playing with her clit, she becomes lost in the moment, moaning and melting into me. Fuck, if it's not the sweetest sound I've ever heard in my life. This girl I've been fantasizing over is moaning as I play with her while she watches something I want to do to her so badly.

Her heart is racing and her breaths are shallow, so I can tell she's about to come. When her entire body locks up, I tilt her head to mine and kiss her for the first time before she lets go of me. I swallow her screams of pleasure because I'm the only one to get those, not anyone else in this room.

As she starts to relax, I reluctantly remove my hand and place her underwear back in place. I keep my mouth on hers as she slowly returns my kiss.

When I pull away, I can tell I've hit her limit tonight. She needs to wrap her head around what's happened. I turn her sideways in my lap, closing her legs, and wrap my arms around her, giving her a safe space to relax. I gently rub my hands up and down her body, soaking in every curve.

Aftercare is important no matter how small the scene, but I've never craved it like this. The need to hold her in my arms and keep her safe is overwhelming.

Finally, Summer sits up and looks around again, but no one is paying us any attention. Just like that, the shy girl I've come to know is back.

"That was amazing, Summer, and I hope you enjoyed yourself." I need to let her know I enjoyed it as much as she did.

She nods with a small smile but looks unsure of what to do next.

"Princess," I say and wait until her eyes are back on me. "I dare you to meet me here again tomorrow night. Same time."

Once again, she nods.

My protective instincts kick in because I can tell she's ready to leave when she looks toward the door. "You drive here?"

"My roommate did. She is getting a ride back later."

"Let me walk you to your car." I stand and take her hand.

"Oh, you don't have to do that." She tries to pull her hand from mine.

"I know I don't. But I want to. I need to make sure you're safe. That hasn't changed. Nothing has to change between us, Summer. We can forget tonight if you want and never mention it again." It's the last thing I want, but I offer it to her anyway. It's the right thing to do for her and for Gemma.

She lets me lead her to the locker area, and I wait for her to get her things and join me back in the hall. Then I walk her out to her car.

"I don't want to forget tonight happened," she says as she turns to me.

"Good, neither do I." I place a soft kiss on her lips and stand back to let her in her car.

After watching her leave, I head home to take care of myself, even though I'm sure my cock wants nothing to do with my hand after having the real thing tonight.

I can't wait to see if she shows up tomorrow.

Chapter 3

Summer

I wake up to the smell of French toast and bacon and know before I even open my eyes that Skye is buttering me up for the details from last night. I knew there was no way of getting around it, and I do need to talk about it to someone. No one else knows I was there last night.

I have no idea what time she got home last night because I was already asleep. Now she's up before me, so I know she wants the details, and there's no way around having the conversation.

I take my time getting ready. I didn't want to wash the night off me, but I took a shower last night. Now my hair is a crazy mess, so I toss it up before going out to find food and coffee waiting for me at the breakfast bar.

Skye is in the kitchen making the last of the French toast. There's homemade blueberry syrup and whipped cream, indicating she's pulled out all the stops. I take a few sips of coffee while Skye plates the last of the food and gives me a knowing glance. She's silent as she works, but the moment her butt hits the chair, she starts with the questions.

"So, what happened? Did you meet someone? Were you able to see the rooms upstairs? Did you go down the Voyeur Hall? See anything you like? Please tell me you didn't bolt the moment I left you."

"I didn't make it out of the main sitting area." Taking my first bite of food, I enjoy how it melts in my mouth.

Skye sighs out loud, and her happiness dies like a balloon deflating. I almost feel bad. "Oh, why not?"

"Because I ran into Gemma's dad."

"Knox? Oh, man, how weird was it?" She's right back into excitement overdrive.

Skye is the one girl who knows how I feel about Knox. I had to tell her so she understood why I didn't want to go over there so much and why Gemma was always over here.

"It wasn't too weird until I was sitting on his lap, and he had me coming in front of everyone there."

"What?" She drops her fork and stares at me with her jaw hanging open.

I've never seen Skye so shocked, and I take a moment to enjoy it.

She listens to my every word without interrupting me. I tell her everything, mostly because I need another opinion.

"What do you want to do? If you want to go tonight, I'll be happy to go with you. I can be a buffer if you need it, or I can drop you off and go."

"I've been thinking about this all night. While I want to go, I don't know if I should. I don't see how this ends any way other than very badly."

"Regardless of what you do, you know you need to call Gemma, right?"

"Knox has kept this part of his life from his daughter for a reason. Do I have the right to tell her about it?"

"If the situation was reversed, would you let her get away with that excuse?"

I hate it when Skye's logic makes sense, especially when I don't want it to, and it doesn't work in my favor.

Gemma is one of those rare people who is a night owl and an early bird. She can stay out partying with the rest of us and be up as late as she wants but still be up super early in the morning, so I don't even bother checking the time before I call her.

She picks up right away, and we spend half an hour on the phone going over what it was like to meet her boyfriend Dustin's parents and what they said and did. She's so happy I don't want to be the one to ruin it.

She gives me plenty of openings where if I had not chickened out, I could have told her what was going on, but I don't. Skye glares at me the whole time because I'm not telling Gemma what happened last night. I avoid eye with her until I hang up the phone.

"This has now turned from a potentially uncomfortable situation to a very bad idea," Skye says, giving me a disapproving look.

"I know, but she's having such a good time meeting Dustin's family. I couldn't ruin it for her. I'll bite the bullet when she's here. I can tell her in person, and she can properly deck me in the face."

I rub my cheek as if Gemma's already punched me. It wouldn't be the first time, but the last time she was drunk, it wasn't at full force and still stung like hell.

Skye frowns. "You should wait to see Knox again. But you're not going to wait, are you?"

Skye knows me too well. I'm not going to wait to see him and not just because of the dare.

Chapter 4

Knox

All day I've been wondering if she's going to show up or if I scared her off. Was it too much, too fast? I've debated calling her to check in but resisted every time. Now here I am waiting on her, and I'm on edge.

One of my favorite things about the club is there's always staff available to teach people and help them learn. Like tonight, they have a demonstration on Shikari, a Japanese rope bondage that's more of an art form.

Though bondage may be my thing, it's a bit complicated for my tastes. But it sure is beautiful to watch. I'm lost in the show until I sense a pair of eyes on me. I slowly scan the room until I find Summer standing with another girl.

She's watching me, so I offer a small smile. She and the girl make their way over. About halfway, the girl she's with stops. She hugs

Summer, says a few words, and goes off to do her thing, leaving Summer alone.

"Who was that?" I nod in the direction the girl left.

"Oh, that's Skye."

I know of her roommate, but I haven't had a chance to meet her yet. I haven't decided if I want to thank her for bringing Summer here or curse her for it. But I guess it will depend on how tonight goes.

"Can I touch you, Princess?" She gives me a shy nod, but that's not good enough. "I need your words."

"Yes, you can touch me."

"Good girl." I take her hand in mine and lead her toward the stage holding the demonstration I was watching earlier. Tables and chairs are placed on one side, but on the other are rows of chairs for those who wish to sit and watch. There's also plenty of standing room.

After grabbing us a table, I order some nachos since I know she loves them, along with some water. After years of observing her, I know she won't eat when she's nervous, and I bet she's been nervous all day.

She shakes her head when the nachos and the water are sent to the table. "Oh, I'm not hungry."

She has a lot to learn. She'll eat when I tell her to eat, but we need to get there slowly.

"It wasn't a question. You need to eat because you're going to need your strength for later." I look at the nachos, and she takes a bite and starts to watch the show. But I can tell when her hunger takes over because she keeps going for bite after bite of the nachos. Once she's done eating, she settles into her chair to watch the rest of the show.

I pull her chair closer and rest an arm on the back. Her side is pressed to mine, and she starts to relax and watch the couple on stage.

I turn my body slightly, resting my other hand on her knee and stroke her soft skin with my thumb. As I slowly move my hand up her leg, I simply watch her. She turns to look at me when I slip my hand under her dress.

"Watch the show, Princess."

Quickly, she turns her eyes back to the stage while I continue to move my hand up her leg. Her legs part slightly for me, and I find her hot pussy and no underwear. I bite back a smile.

"Naughty girl," I whisper in her ear.

"Easier access," she smirks.

There's the sassy girl who's always kept me on my toes.

She's already wet before I begin to stroke her. I had a feeling she'd like the show. Bondage seems to excite her, and this rope play is a beautiful version of it.

When I rub her clit, she starts squirming in her seat. "Knox!" she moans.

"Look around. People are having sex two tables over. The show is meant to be a turn-on, and everyone is indulging."

Her eyes roam the room and her gaze snags on the woman sitting on the table while her partner eats her out. Neither of them seems to care about the show, instead putting on one of their own.

"Eyes back on the stage," I command.

Summer obeys so perfectly, and I reward her by thrusting two fingers into her, causing her to gasp.

"Keep quiet," I whisper into her ear as I continue thrusting my fingers in and out of her, strumming her clit with my thumb.

One of her hands grips my thigh and squeezes harder the closer she gets. She tries to clamp her legs together, but it doesn't stop me. The moment her climax rushes over her, her head drops back, and she squeezes her eyes shut. Her mouth closes tight, trying hard to be as quiet as possible. At that moment, I can't help thinking how beautiful she is.

Her pussy grips my fingers and coats them in her juices. My cock aches as she opens her dazed eyes and focuses on me. Keeping eye contact, I bring my hand to my mouth and lick every drop of her from my fingers before putting her dress back in place.

"Come on. I rented a room upstairs." I take her hand, and she follows me on wobbly legs.

I hold her to my side on the short elevator ride to the second floor. But I don't give her time to look around the smaller lounge area as I almost drag her to the room I rented. Once I scan my card, I pull us in, closing us inside.

Needing to slow things down, I take a step back. But her gasp draws my attention. She slowly walks to the floor-to-ceiling windows overlooking the area we were just in.

"They're one-way windows, but I can close them altogether if you'd like."

She watches everyone down below for a moment before she turns back to me and offers one of her shy smiles.

"Yes, I think I'd like the window closed."

I move to the wall panel, and with the push of a button, the glass turns black, obscuring the view.

Finally, she turns away from the glass and looks around the room. To one side is a large bed, and the Saint Andrews cross is on the other. There are shelves of toys, a closet full of clothes, and several mirrors in one of the corners. There's also a small seating area in front of the windows.

"Do you remember your safe words?"

"Green means good, yellow means you're hitting one of my limits or coming close to it, and red means stop."

"Very good. And what are your limits, Princess?"

She looks around the room, lost in thought, and as much as I want to hurry her up, this is an important conversation we need to have. I'm already taking things too far, so I want her to know that at least I did it the right way, even though I shouldn't be doing this with my daughter's best friend.

"I'm not sure. No blood play, and I'm not much into pain. The ball gags hold no appeal to me. But I don't know." She shrugs, unable to meet my eyes.

"Eyes on me, Princess." I wait until she is looking at me again. "Do you want this?"

"Yes," she whispers.

"Then I'm willing to learn and test your limits with you, so long as you are honest and vocal about it. Understood?"

"Yes..."

I can tell there's more she wants to say, and I know I'm pushing my luck, but I'm going to do it. "Yes, Daddy," I correct her.

Her eyes go wide, and she smiles.

"I plan to take good care of you, Princess. You'll see."

Taking a deep breath, I step into the Dom she has yet to see. "Now go take off your clothes and climb on the bed," I tell her in a "don't mess with me" voice.

Her eyes snap to mine, but she doesn't move.

"Don't make me tell you again."

This time she moves quickly and pulls her dress over her head, revealing she's wearing nothing underneath. She sits on the edge of the bed and removes her shoes before settling herself with her back to the headboard.

I walk to one of the cabinets and rub my fingers over all the different bindings but settle on the soft silk. "Remember your safe words. Now lie down in the center of the bed."

Once she's in position, I move to the head of the bed and tie her arms to the headboard before standing back and fully admiring her naked body spread open for me.

Chapter 5

Summer

If I had my hands free, my first instinct would be to cover myself. With his eyes on me, I'm exposed and a little self-conscious, despite how he's looking at me, so hungry and full of desire as if I'm a tasty treat. No one has ever looked at me the way Knox is looking at me now.

He walks back to the cabinet and gets two more pieces of black silk, and moves to tie my legs to the bed. When I fight to keep my legs closed, he looks at me.

"Do you want to use your safe word?"

There's no way I want him to stop, but handing over this kind of control to someone, especially my best friend's father, is extremely nerve-wracking. Allowing myself to be spread open and vulnerable is a little scary.

"No, I don't."

"Then spread your legs for me, little girl."

Since we got into this room, his voice has been different. It's not the friendly tone I've known from Knox all these years. It's commanding and stern. There's no way I won't obey him. I couldn't if I tried.

Following his orders, I spread one leg toward him. He ties the black silk around my ankle and pulls my leg even wider as he ties the other end around the bed. Moving to the other side, he does the same with my other foot, leaving me wide open for him to look at or do whatever he would like.

The thought of him having complete access to me and doing whatever he wants has my blood rushing and my pussy gushing. He can see how wet I am. There's no way for me to hide now.

"What are your safe words?"

I take a deep breath. "Green for good, yellow if I'm getting close to hitting a limit, and red to stop."

"Very good. I'm not going to ask you again." He moves to another cabinet and pulls out something I can't see in the dim lighting before walking back to the bed and sitting down.

Closing my eyes, I wait with bated breath for him to touch me, praying he does. But when I open my eyes, he's holding a feather. He starts at my neck, lightly running it over each of my breasts, causing me to gasp with the sensation. When he circles it over my belly button and down my sides, I burst out in giggles. Apparently, he knows how ticklish I am.

"I love the sound of that giggle. When you were over with Gemma, you two would be in her room giggling about stuff. I could have listened all day. You had no idea how hard my cock was while you were giggling upstairs. Did you?"

"No," I whisper.

He sets the feather down and traces the same path with his finger. "And all those summers you spent by my pool in that skimpy bathing suit, you had no idea how much you were teasing me, did you?" He pinches my nipple and looks up at me, expecting an answer.

"No," I whisper again.

"You have no idea how many times I stood in my room watching you lie out there tanning. And still, you have no idea how hard it made me and how many times my cum coated my wall watching you. Do you?"

He pinches my other nipple, causing me to gasp with the exquisite pain. Unable to speak the words this time, I shake my head. Trembling with anticipation, I wait to see what he does next.

His lips trail down my neck to my breasts and over to my nipples, where he bites each one. I cry out, but he continues to kiss down my stomach to my thighs, where he bites the inside of each one. A flash of pain hits me before pleasure follows.

Goosebumps race across my skin as my best friend's dad has his head between my thighs, and all I can think is I want more.

Knox situates himself and starts sucking my clit, using his thumbs to open me wide. Leisurely, he licks every inch of me, sending shivers over every inch of my body. When he sucks on my clit again with the perfect pressure, I give in to the waves of pleasure rolling off me. Screaming his name, I fall over the edge. I want to move, but the silk holds me in place.

His gaze is focused on me when I finally open my eyes again. "Do you still want this?"

"Yes." I don't hesitate.

"I'm not using a condom," he says, climbing over me. "If we do this, you will be mine. I am your daddy."

Of course, I agree, as there's no scenario where I don't want to be his.

"I had plans to tease you and drag this out, but somehow you know what to say to drive me mad," he says, almost like he is angry before he slams into me so hard it steals my breath.

He gives me a brief second to adjust before he starts moving, and the pain quickly transforms into pleasure. "Fuck, you are so tight, Princess. You feel so good. Like you were made for Daddy's cock."

I can't form words. I moan as he stretches and fills me in a way I never thought possible. The harder he thrusts, the more I moan. I didn't think rough sex was something I'd like, but he's hitting all the right places. When one of his hands slides between us and plays with my clit, I'm a goner.

My entire body locks up as the orgasm hits me full force, unlike anything I've experienced before. I barely register him groaning in my ear as his hot cum coats me from the inside and another smaller orgasm hits me.

I think I black out because the next thing I know, my hands are free, and Knox is untying my legs. He curls up behind me on the bed and pulls me into his arms, rubbing my wrists where the black silk was holding them in place.

Neither of us says anything as he holds me, kissing my shoulder and rubbing his hand up and down my arm.

What are you supposed to say during after-care? *Hey, thanks for the hot, rough sex. See you next time.*

I choose not to say anything because I don't want to break the spell he's woven over me. And I don't want him to kick me out and send me on my way. I want to enjoy being in his arms a little longer.

"I think aftercare just became one of my favorite things. Being able to hold you in my arms like this, I didn't think I would crave it so badly," he says as if reading my thoughts.

Snuggling into his arms some more, we enjoy a comfortable and easy silence. But I don't want to overstay my welcome or make things weird, so after the feeling returns to my legs and I'm sure I can stand on both feet, I climb out of bed and get dressed.

He sits in bed watching me with his muscles on full display and only the thinnest of sheets covering his waist. "I dare you to come to my house and spend the day by the pool with me tomorrow."

Another dare and another reason to spend time with him. He isn't the only one with pool-side fantasies I wouldn't mind living out while our time together lasts.

"Well, I guess you'll find out tomorrow. I'm not sure if it's a dare I'm going to take or not." I grab the rest of my things, offer him a smile, and turn and walk out the door.

Chapter 6

Knox

As I wait for Summer to arrive, I make sure I have all her favorite snacks and prepare her favorite lunch—my homemade baked macaroni and cheese. I have her favorite drink in the fridge, Dr. Pepper, and the Hershey Kisses she loves in the pantry.

Gemma is out of town spending time with her new boyfriend's family, and I'm happy about that. I think Summer and I need this time, just the two of us, without worrying about what to say to Gemma.

Last night, I realized this isn't some fling. After showing her around Club Red, I have no intention of letting her walk away from me, nor am I walking away. All this time, I've been denying myself, and now I've had this taste of Summer, there's no possibility of leaving her.

While waiting, I call my buddy Grant, who recently got married to his son's ex-girlfriend. They live out in Vegas, and he owns several of the hotels and casinos out there. When I attended their wedding, it was amazing to see the love the two of them share. But what I'm interested in is knowing how he broke it to his son. It's not a conversation I'm looking forward to with Gemma, and I need to tread lightly.

"Hey, Knox, what's going on?" Grant answers the phone.

We spend a few minutes catching up on what's happening in our lives with him in Las Vegas and me in Chicago. Unfortunately, we don't get to see each other as much as we'd like.

"So, I have a question for you," I say, trying to start the conversation.

"I'm an open book. What's on your mind?"

"How did you break it to your son that you were with his ex-girlfriend?"

Grant's quiet for a minute. When he doesn't say anything, I decide to fill him in on the details.

"I may have started something with my daughter's best friend, and I need to know how to bring it up to Gemma in the best way possible. Because there's no way I'm walking away from Summer."

"Since you've made up your mind, that's a big part of it. I never told him the way I wanted to. He walked in, and it came down to me having to be open and honest about my feelings. It was weird for him for a while, but he was happy for us in the end. Be firm and don't waver. Any insecurity, and she'll jump on it."

Just then, the doorbell rings, and my heart races. Summer has arrived. I thank Grant for his advice and get off the phone to answer the door.

Summer is wearing cut-off jean shorts showcasing those long sleek legs and a tank top. Beneath it, I can see her bathing suit. It's a teal blue bikini with all that gorgeous tan skin exposed. Not only should it be illegal, but it drives me crazy.

"Head out to the pool and relax. I'll join you soon."

I'm in jeans and a button-down shirt. It's something casual I would wear to work because I'm going to play out this fantasy that's been on my mind a lot longer than it should have been. After taking a deep breath, I go out to the back porch as if I'm getting home from work.

I find Summer stripped down to her bathing suit and swimming in the water. The huge smile lighting up her face sets my soul at ease. She's healthy, happy, and safe, which is all I could ever ask for.

"Have you put on sunscreen?" I ask as I walk up to the edge of the pool.

I can see the slight blush on her cheeks as she swims over to meet me.

"Get out and sit down. I'll go grab some sunscreen."

I run into the house to grab it, knowing she's horrible at remembering to put it on. When I get back, she's sitting on the lounge chair.

Sitting beside her, I put the suntan lotion on her back, shoulders, and neck. Taking my time, I massage the tension from her neck and shoulders before squirting more lotion into my hand. I reach around her, rubbing lotion on her chest before slipping my hand under the triangles over her breasts.

"I... I don't think... you should be touching me there," she says, feeding into my fantasy without me having to tell her.

"Lie down so I can get lotion on the rest of you."

Obediently, she does as I ask. I start at her feet and spread lotion onto her legs. As I get to her upper thighs, I rub up to the edge of her swimsuit bottoms but only give her a few light grazes of my hand. I slowly move up and rub lotion onto her flat stomach, covering every inch of her in lotion. The last thing I need is for my girl to get any hint of a sunburn.

Once I've rubbed in all the lotion, I let my hand lazily trail under her bikini, and I find her like I want her—wet. She clamps her legs together, gasping, and her eyes go wide.

"Have to make sure every inch of you is covered. Can't have you getting sunburned if your swimsuit slips, can we?" I ask as I run a finger through her folds.

"No, we can't have that," she pants.

Her legs relax enough so I can pry one finger into her. "It would be uncomfortable to get sunburn on this beautiful pussy. Wouldn't it? We can't let that happen." I add a second finger, and she moans, letting her head fall back.

I use my thumb to play with her clit while thrusting two fingers in and out of her, using my other hand to pull the triangle of fabric covering her round breasts to the side.

"Double-checking to make sure I got these beautiful tits covered," I say as I pinch one of her nipples and pull it taut before letting go.

Like last night that little bit of pain gets her even wetter. I do the same to the other nipple and press harder on her clit.

"Come for me, Princess. We can use that cream to protect your pussy. Come on Daddy's hand." I growl and pinch her nipple one more time, sending her into an orgasm. Screw the neighbors. I don't try to stop her screams of pleasure. Hell, I'm enjoying them.

As she relaxes, I put her swimsuit back in place and lick my fingers clean of her juices. I can't let it go to waste.

Without a word, I get up and make a plate for lunch. She eats it with a lazy smile on her face the whole time. When she's done, I take her plate and head inside to clean it up and save the leftovers.

By the time I come back outside, she is lying on her stomach, and her bathing suit is untied to prevent tan lines. Her delectable bare ass is on display, and I lose it.

Chapter 7

Summer

How many times did I lie out here trying to tease him and hoping for some kind of reaction? Even in front of Gemma. I never thought I'd get one, but it seems I did. I just didn't see it.

Since it's only us, I decide to push my luck. After last night, I'm sure to get a reaction from him. So, as I lay on my stomach on the lounge chair, I reach around and untie my bikini top to avoid tan lines.

Untying my bikini bottom, I leave them in place but make them as small as possible. They're almost like a thong, but I'll be able to get as much sun as possible. Then I lie there and wait for Knox.

The sun feels so good on my skin, and I got next to no sleep last night as I thought over every detail of being with Knox in that private room. That must be why I don't hear the back door or his approaching footsteps.

A hand presses on the back of my head, holding me down. "Look at you. Are you lying here begging for a cock to fill you, Princess?" Knox growls as he rips away my bikini bottoms and forces my legs apart.

His calling me Princess calms me, and I sink into the lounge chair. He takes that as a yes.

"Well, I guess that's what I'll have to give you," he says, filling me with one solid thrust.

The pain of being forcibly stretched so fast quickly fades. I was plenty wet from his playtime earlier, and this is exactly what I wanted. Now it's time to play my role.

"What are you doing? We shouldn't be doing this," I gasp.

"What did you think was going to happen when you untied that sad excuse of a bathing suit and laid yourself on this chair like an offering? Any man walking by would have taken you. Just be happy it was me." He leans over my body and whispers the last part in my ear.

He's thrusting so hard that the chair is scraping across the concrete on his patio.

"But what about the neighbors? They could see us!"

"That's what you wanted, isn't it, little girl? For the neighbors to see you and to make their cocks hard. Drive them crazy as they watched you tanning and me rubbing lotion all over this young, gorgeous body while they knew they couldn't have you. But I'm having you, aren't I?" Making his point, he thrusts into me harder.

"Yes, Daddy."

"Don't worry about your friend finding us, either. If you come fast enough, I can be out of you, and you can be back to sunning yourself before she gets back out here. She never has to know you're full of my cum."

He tugs my face toward him using my hair while his other hand snakes between me and the lounger to play with my clit. All at once, he stops moving, removes his hand from my clit, and lies over me. With his face next to me, he says, "You are mine. Princess. Do you understand? Nothing is going to change it. Not when Gemma gets home, not anyone's reaction to us, and not just when we're in the club. Do you understand me?"

I nod, but he pulls my head back a bit more. "Use your 'big girl' words."

Fuck, why is that such a turn-on? "Yes, Daddy, I understand. I'm yours."

His lips crash into mine, but he doesn't start moving again. His hips pin me to the chair so I can't get any friction. "That goes both ways. I'm yours too, Princess. Only yours."

Without giving me a chance to respond, he starts thrusting into me again, and the orgasm I thought had faded roars to life as strong as ever.

He knows it, too, because he plays my body expertly. He angles his hips, giving me the right amount of pain to my clit, and I orgasm harder than I ever have. His lips are on me again as he swallows my screams. It's a good thing because I couldn't stop if I tried.

Knox grunts and holds himself inside me. His warm cum fills me, making my walls clench on him, milking him, needing every last drop.

By the time we're both done, my bones have turned to jello, and I'm not sure I'll ever move again. Knox stands and pulls on his swim trunks, grabs the towel I brought, and wraps me in it. He carries me inside and up the stairs. I rest my head on his shoulder, loving being in his arms.

Knox takes me straight into the shower, sets me on his shower bench, and turns on the water. As I watch him languidly, he grabs a washcloth and adds his body wash. He moves to the panel, presses some buttons, and the showerhead turns off, but water falls from the ceiling. The warm water washing over my back is wonderful.

He kneels in front of me, taking the now wet towel and tossing it to the far corner of the shower. With efficient moves, he removes my swimsuit, leaving me completely exposed.

Once I'm naked, he starts with my shoulders and washes every part of me, not playing or teasing but slowly taking care of me. It's not meant to be sexual or to excite me, but it does. My nipples are hard, and I know I'm wet, but he ignores it. After he's finished, he rinses off all the soap and removes the tie from my hair.

He leans my head back into the spray and runs his hands gently through my hair, untangling it as he lets the water wash over it. When he's finished, he turns off the water and gets a towel. It's warm and toasty and feels good as he dries me off.

Wrapping me in another warm towel, he carries me into his large walk-in closet. There's a center island the height of a kitchen counter, and he sets me on it. He grabs one of his shirts and pulls it over my head before he tugs on a pair of sweatpants.

Finally, he carries me to his bed and places me under the covers before he finally speaks. "You okay with what happened, Princess?"

I snuggle up to his side. "Mm, very okay with it. It was hot as hell and a fantasy of mine for sure."

He chuckles and runs his hand up and down my arm. "One of my fantasies too. Are you telling me you've been purposely teasing me all these years?" He eyes me suspiciously.

I hug him a bit harder. "Why is it so hard to believe? I've had a crush on you since Gemma's sixteenth birthday party."

"I was way too old for you then. Hell, I still am. There's no way a beautiful young woman like you had a crush on an old man like me. Besides, you were dating that football player at the party. I remember it clearly. I didn't like him one bit. He was too cocky, and his friend had his eyes on Gemma. I had my eyes on the two of you all night."

"I remember you came out, took off your shirt, and got in the pool. That was the day I knew there was something different about you. Every time I looked up, you were looking at me, and it made me feel things I hadn't felt before. A week later, I dumped the football player."

Knox is quiet, but his hand never stops moving as he rubs my arm, my back, and any place he can reach. It's a comforting movement. Is he thinking of that party like I am?

"I was thankful when you two stopped hanging out with the football players. The guy you went to prom with wasn't so bad."

My prom date and I had been friends since kindergarten. Even though I had a ton of guys ask me out, I figured going with a friend was my safe bet since many of them were more interested in whether I would put out.

Until I went to college, I played it safe. But in college, I had a serious boyfriend, lost my virginity, and had all those firsts. Through it all, I thought this silly crush was over until I came back into town and saw Knox again.

"He was a nice guy. A little too nice, I guess. I dated a bit in college, but none of them made me feel like you have in the past few days."

There's a break in the conversation, and he's quiet, thinking about what he wants to say next. But it's not an uncomfortable silence.

"Gemma's mom and I were high school sweethearts. She ended up pregnant, and we got married because that's what you did. We had a long ride, but we were more friends who had a child together than anything else. We made it work for Gemma's sake, and I took care of them."

I want to hear what Knox has to say, so I remain silent. Gemma doesn't talk about her mother. She died when she was young, and Gemma doesn't remember much about her. I never pry because it seems a touchy subject for her, yet I would like to know more.

"When Gemma was six, her mother was killed in a car accident. Hit by a drunk driver. I couldn't grieve her like she deserved. I grieved her as a friend, not as the love of my life. Gemma doesn't talk about her much, and that's probably my fault. I found Club Red a few years ago. The club was enough for me, and I never felt the need to date, so there hasn't been anyone serious. Instead, I focused on raising Gemma. I love that girl, but she was a wild child, as I'm sure you probably remember."

I do remember. Gemma's a risk-taker and a daredevil, but a good person and one of the best people I know. I have a sudden urgency to make sure Knox knows that too.

"She was a risk-taker back then. Not so much anymore, but she still loves to push her boundaries. She respects you, and she didn't do drugs or sleep around. She was a good person and didn't care about being popular. If someone was bullied, she was the first to help. Often she'd give up her lunch to some kid who needed it."

We talk a bit more, and I drift off to sleep at some point. I don't know how long I nap, but I sense Knox's gaze on me before I open my eyes. He's leaning up on his elbow, watching me.

"This isn't a dare for me or something temporary from the club," he says.

"It's not a dare for me either," I admit.

"I want all of you, Summer. This isn't a fling. You are mine, and I'm not letting you go. I love you. Have for a long time now."

My eyes sting with tears because this isn't how I expected today to be. "I love you too," I tell him and pull him in for a kiss.

"Stay the night. Gemma gets back tomorrow evening, so we'll have one last night together before we tell her about us."

I agree. Knox spends the night making love to me and giving every inch of my skin attention. Driving me crazy in the best way.

Chapter 8

Knox

As I wake up, the smell of coffee and bacon fills the air. For a moment, I think Summer is up before me making breakfast, but when I open my eyes, she's still sound asleep beside me. I enjoy the sight of her in my bed for a little longer before getting up. I dress and head downstairs to see who's cooking breakfast. Normally I'd say it's my daughter, but she isn't here. Maybe it's my buddy Grant, who isn't supposed to be in town but has a key to my house.

I find Gemma and her boyfriend in the kitchen. "I thought you two weren't getting back in until tonight," I say as I walk in and pull my daughter in for a hug.

Gemma has a huge smile on her face. "We weren't. But we were able to get an earlier flight, so we thought we'd surprise you. We have something to tell you."

I send up a silent prayer that she's not pregnant. "Oh, yeah?"

I pour myself a cup of coffee to buy some time before I turn back to look at them. When I do, my daughter holds up her hand. She has an engagement ring on her finger, a decent-sized one too.

I stand there in complete shock. They've only recently started dating, and I only met him for the first time a few weeks ago. Further, he never talked to me about this and didn't ask for my blessing. Not that he needs it, but it would have been a nice gesture, especially with how new the relationship is and how close my daughter and I are. Something about it rubs me the wrong way.

I pull her in for a hug. "If you're happy, I'm happy, sweetheart."

I don't want to ruin this moment for her. I can process my feelings on it later. I want her to be happy, and I don't want to overshadow this moment, but Summer is sleeping upstairs, so this talk can't wait.

"I have some news too. And I hope you can be happy for me," I begin.

"Oh, my God! Did you finally meet someone? Can I meet her?" Gemma is more excited than she was a moment ago. She claps her hands and does a little dance, eager to meet the new woman in my life.

"Yes, but—"

Summer walks into the kitchen wearing nothing but my shirt. Her hair's a mess, and there's no hiding that she's slept over.

She sees Gemma and her boyfriend and freezes. Her eyes go wide as she looks at me. Her look begs me to tell her what to do and how to handle this situation because that's my role with her. Giving her direction is what I'm supposed to do.

I walk to Summer's side and wrap my arm around her waist, pulling her to me. All the excitement on Gemma's face has vanished, and she looks angrier than when she found out her football player boyfriend cheated on her with the cheerleader.

"Are you kidding me? Summer is the new girl? She's my best friend and way too fucking young for you, don't you think? And seriously, Summer, my dad? Don't you think he's been through enough in his life without you doing this to him? What the hell were you thinking?" Gemma's voice is full of disgust.

I can't believe those words came from my daughter, and her anger is enough to send Summer into tears. She rips herself away from me and runs upstairs.

"I think the two of you should stay at Dustin's house," I say, keeping my voice neutral because I don't want to say something I might regret later.

Pure shock crosses Gemma's face. "You're kicking me out of my own house?"

"No, I'm kicking you out of *my* house and soon to be Summer's house. You will never talk to her like that again. Be gone by the time I come back, and thank you for breakfast."

I head for the stairs but stop to look at Dustin. "You and I will talk later, as we should have before you promised to spend the rest of your life with my daughter." I turn and go up after Summer. I don't need her getting any ideas that things have changed between us.

When I get back up to my room, Summer is already dressed in the clothes she was wearing yesterday. She moves frantically around the bedroom, gathering up all her stuff and packing it into the tote she brought with her.

Walking to her, I wrap my arms around her waist and halt her movements. I won't have her thinking she's going to leave me. "I'm sorry. I didn't know they were coming home early. I was getting ready to tell them about you when you walked in. Gemma was way out of line, but I sent her Dustin's to cool off."

"She's the nicest person I know, but I've never seen her so upset or mean toward anyone, much less me. I knew she'd be upset, but I never thought she'd act like that. This is why I was scared to make a move. Her friendship means so much to me. She was my only friend when I needed someone and didn't have anyone. She's always been there. I can't imagine my life without her."

Summer breaks free from my hold, grabs her bag, and before I can even register what she's said and what's going on, she's out the door.

Chapter 9

Summer

When I get home, I'm thankful to find Skye there. She takes one look at me and pulls the ice cream out of the freezer along with two spoons, and we both collapse on the couch. I tell her everything from the last couple of days, from how I've fallen for Knox to what Gemma said.

Skye knows Gemma because she's constantly over here. The three of us often hang out, and even Skye is shocked at her reaction. "My guess is it came as a huge shock, and as things calm down and she realizes what happened, she'll feel differently. I know she wants both of you happy."

I don't say anything because I hope she's right. We end up watching TV and talking while we finish the ice cream and simply sit together. Finally, she wraps her arms around me and holds me because what else can she do? At some point, I drift off to sleep and wake up to my phone going off.

Checking it, I see Knox is calling me and ignore it. A few moments later, Gemma calls me, but I ignore it too.

I shower, get dressed, and try to get some social media work done, hoping a distraction will make things easier. When that doesn't work, I decide to get out of the house. Since we ate all the ice cream last night, I head to the store and get some more. Before I leave, I let Skye know where I'm going. It feels good to get out of the house among strangers, people who have no idea what's going on in my life and honestly could care less.

By the time I get home, Skye has gone to work, and Gemma is sitting on my front porch. Knowing I can't avoid this talk forever, I open the door and invite her in.

"I'm not happy about this, but after you left, I was talking with my dad," Gemma begins as soon as we're inside. "I've never seen him so happy as when he talks about you. How did this happen? Couldn't someone have told me the truth?"

"Neither of us set out for this to happen. But you might not want to know the details." I try to be honest.

"You're my best friend, and from how my dad is talking, it looks like you're about to be my stepmom. So I think I have a right to know."

Of course, she's going to play the best friend card. I hope Knox will forgive me for telling her the whole truth because I'm sure this is a part of his life he never wanted her to know about.

"After I finished that big project at work, Skye demanded I get out of the house. I didn't want to because you weren't here. I had no desire to go out and do anything, but Skye said she'd take me to this club she was sure I'd like."

"My dad never struck me as a club-goer," Gemma says with a confused look.

"Skye took me to Club Red. I had a drink and was standing there looking around. She'd gone off with one of her friends, and up walks your dad. He gave me a tour of the place, more as a way to protect me than anything. And one thing led to another. We realized we were attracted to each other but never would have made a move if it hadn't been for that night at the club."

I leave out the intimate details because even though she's my best friend, it's still her father we're talking about.

"So, this all happened a few days ago? It's not serious?"

"You and I have known each other for years. During that time, your father and I also got to know each other. While we may have acted on this attraction recently, it's been coming for some time. It's serious. He said he loves me, and I love him."

Gemma is quiet for a few minutes, and I know she's thinking about what to say next. In that way, she's like her dad. "Is that why you stopped coming over and we started hanging out over here?"

"Yes, it was too hard being over there. I was worried you'd catch on, and I hated how distracted I was when he was home and how distracted I was when he wasn't. I wondered where he was, so it was easier to be here instead."

Gemma doesn't say anything, but she nods, and after a moment, she reaches for me and pulls me into one of her tight hugs. "I'm so sorry for how I reacted. I was in shock and didn't deal with it well. While I want both of you to be happy, I never expected it would be the both of you together. Hell, I never saw him date, so I had no idea what his type was. Do you think we can forget the whole issue with the club? That would be great."

I hug her back because I want nothing more than to have my best friend back and be on good terms again. Her friendship means more to me than anything.

"But I won't be calling you mom, and you better not hurt him because I will take his side. Don't get me involved in your fights, at least for a while. Let's keep PDA to a minimum until I get used to all this. That is if I can get used to it."

I laugh because I don't know what else to say. Even though I walked out, Knox didn't stop me. Other than the one phone call, he hasn't tried to come after me. I don't know if I've screwed up my chances, but it's not something I'm going to burden her with right now.

"Tell me about this engagement. How did he ask you? Let me see the ring." I try to shift the attention back to her.

Gemma's smile quickly turns to a frown. "My dad said Dustin never talked to him about proposing to me. I always imagined the guy I married would have enough respect for my dad to at least talk to him and get his blessing. It's not like I have anyone else but my dad. Dustin should understand how important he is to me."

"Is that a deal-breaker for you?"

I have a feeling it's a question she's been avoiding. "I don't know. It doesn't seem right to me. Maybe I got wrapped up in the whirlwind of it all and him proposing. I don't think I've had time to digest it. So, I'm going to let it sit for a bit and not make any plans or set a date. After some reflection, I'll see how I feel about it.

"I think it's best to give it a few days. Right now, it's new and shiny. Let it wear off and think about how your life will be with him. What is he planning for his life, and does it match your hopes and dreams?"

"You're already giving me motherly advice. I don't know if I can stand it," Gemma jokes. She stands and pulls me in for a hug before heading to the door.

"You need to talk to my dad and make this right because he's miserable." With that, she's gone, leaving and in an empty house with my mind racing.

Chapter 10

Knox

I pace in the living room, not sure of my next move. Gemma told me she was going to talk to Summer, and I have no idea how it's going. Neither is answering their phone, and I'm minutes away from storming my way over there.

If Summer doesn't talk to me, I can't fix this. On the phone, it's too easy to hang up on me. If we're face to face, I can make her hear me and use any means necessary to get her to understand she isn't getting rid of me this easily.

I'm grabbing my car keys as Gemma walks in the door. She gives me a strange look and sets her stuff down with no hint of how the conversation went.

"So?" I need the details, and I want to demand them from her, but I know I need to be careful about our relationship. Over time, Gemma will come around. But if I don't move soon, I could lose Summer forever.

"We talked about more than you. It was needed and good for both of us. Things are okay but weird. I mean a sex club, Dad?" She cringes and goes into the kitchen.

I follow as she gets something to drink. I can't think of trying to eat or drink anything right now. "So, she told you everything?"

I don't care if she did. Summer needs someone to talk to, and Gemma has always been that for her. I don't want their relationship to change, as weird as it might get at times. Summer loves my daughter for who she is, and that's a big part of what drew me to her.

Growing up, Gemma would make friends only to find out they wanted something from her because of the money associated with my family name. They tossed her aside when they realized we didn't spend money and lived a modest life.

Later, she made friends who dropped her for silly things like they didn't have the same taste in music or her blue hair was too wild. Her hair is her natural color now, but Summer is the only one who still supports Gemma no matter how crazy her ideas are.

Gemma cringes again. "Summer told me a lot. But not *everything*. We decided certain... ugh, details could go unsaid. But we have very few secrets, so yeah, she told me all the important stuff."

I can't help but laugh. We've always been close but never close enough to talk about my love life, much less my sex life, and we don't talk about hers either. I know when she lost her virginity and to who, but the information flow stops there.

"If this ends badly, I'm screwed. You're my dad, and she's my best friend. Actually, she might as well be my sister at this point. I won't choose sides despite what I led her to believe, and you'll have to be okay with that."

"It's not going to end badly. I plan to marry her as soon as I can get her to agree. How do you feel about that?" I cross my arms and lean against the dining room table, watching her.

Gemma falls silent for a moment, and I appreciate the thought she's putting into her answer, even if I hate to wait for an answer.

"Honestly, I feel better about you marrying her than I do about marrying Dustin."

I don't say anything. I don't need to because that speaks volumes. But it's a decision she has to make herself. I know we'll be okay when she walks over and gives me a hug.

Before she heads upstairs, she turns back to me. "Give her time to get her head around all this. She'll come to you, but be patient."

"How can you be sure?" I ask uncertainly.

"Because I'm the one person who knows her better than you do." She smiles and goes upstairs.

Gemma's right. I try to be patient, but my mind is on Summer. I can't work, check social media, or concentrate long enough to read. Nothing on TV helps either.

Gemma makes dinner and talks to me to try to take my mind off it, but she finally gives up and pays attention to her phone. Even though I try to eat, my stomach rejects all food.

After helping clean up the kitchen, I decide enough is enough. I'm going to go after her. No sooner have I decided than my phone pings with a text.

Summer: Come find me.

The photo attached is the outside Club Red.

"I'm going out!" I yell to Gemma and run to my room to get dressed.

"Bring her home, Dad."

"That's the plan. Can't promise it won't be awkward."

"I'll make breakfast." She winks, and I head out.

In record time, I'm at the club. I can't take my phone inside, so I go in, hoping to find her at the bar. No such luck. Scanning the main room, I spot the girl she was here with the other night, her roommate Skye.

I walk up to her. "Hey, where's Summer?"

Skye smiles and doesn't hide that she's checking me out. "Now that would be cheating. I will say you're not on the right floor, though." She turns back to the man she was talking to.

I run for the stairs, not bothering with the elevator, checking the second-floor lounge and each playroom. On my right are the themed playrooms and on my left are the rooms people rent out or leave open for others to join. I check all that aren't closed off.

I find her in one of the empty rooms on my left, strapped to a St. Andrew's Cross, naked. I close the door and windows because she's only for me. "Who strapped you up here, Princess?"

"Skye."

I remove my shoes and shirt as I admire her stretched out on the cross, open and ready for me. Her nipples are hard, and I can tell she's wet for me, even from across the room in low light.

"And what was your plan if someone else walked into the room?"

"I had someone outside who made sure that didn't happen. One of Skye's friends."

I will never know how I missed him, but I'll thank him later.

I can tell by the look in her eyes she wants to play. I can give her that because we'll have plenty of time to talk when I get her home and in my bed.

We spend all night talking about our relationship, kids, the future, and where we see ourselves in five and ten years.

Before the night is over, I know what she wants to do now she's got her degree and what types of books she likes to read. We made love between it all before finally falling asleep.

I smell breakfast downstairs. It's time to wake her up and try to find our new normal. "Princess, time to get up. Gemma made breakfast for us." I push her hair out of her face.

She groans and opens her eyes. "Too tired," she mumbles.

"Let's get up and talk to Gemma, and I'll make time for you to nap today."

"Will you be in bed with me?"

"I promise I will."

She sighs as she finally gets up and goes to the bathroom. Once we're both dressed, we head downstairs.

"Hey! Coffee is on, and food will be ready soon. Summer, I made the pancakes you like," Gemma calls over her shoulder, not looking at us.

As I pass her on my way to get coffee, I kiss the top of her head. "Thank you, sweetheart."

Once we're sitting down to eat, the girls start talking about people they know. It's like any other morning when Summer has been here, except this time, my hand is on her thigh, and when she looks at me, her smile reaches her eyes.

Once we're done, I know it's now or never. "So, I know things will take some getting used to around here, but I figure I should put all my cards on the table."

Standing, I push my chair out of the way and drop to one knee in front of Summer. She gasps, but from the corner of my eyes, I can see Gemma has a huge smile lighting her face.

"I tried to hide my feelings for so long, but when I saw you at Club Red and touched you for the first time, I knew there was no going back."

Matter of fact, I knew it so much that the following morning I went and bought the ring I now pull out of my pocket. "I want to marry you and spend the rest of my life taking care of you, playing with you, and loving you. So, I have one more dare for you. I dare you to marry me."

Summer looks at Gemma, who nods, and she looks back at me. "Yes!"

She doesn't hesitate, and I slide on the ring in a blur and pull her into my arms.

I have never loved a good dare quite so much.

Epilogue

Summer

Six Months Later

It feels like an understatement to say the last six months have been the best of my life, but they have.

Gemma decided not to marry Dustin, and I don't remember the last time I saw her so happy. It was like a weight lifted off her shoulders when they parted ways.

I moved in with Knox the same day he proposed, and Gemma moved in with Skye, so she had some space from us. It's worked out great because I don't feel bad about leaving Skye without a roommate, and Skye even took Gemma to Club Red.

Less than a month after he proposed, Knox and I got married. We waited because I fell in love with this amazing dress, and it took that long to get it ready for me due to all the lace details.

Knox whisked me away for a two-month honeymoon, and we visited several popular BDSM clubs in New York City, London, and Paris. But when we came home, we still felt most at home in Club Red and decided to keep our membership there—though we coordinate with Gemma so we don't end up there on the same nights. Besides, we only go a few times a month now, and we're thinking of putting in a playroom at the house and only visiting the Club for special events like tonight.

Since the night I was strapped to the St. Andrew's Cross, I've been obsessed with it. The complete control Knox has over me and the amount of trust shared between us is wonderful. We both love it.

But tonight, we take it to the next level. I'm nervous, but we've been working up to this for months. I'll be tied to the St. Andrew's Cross is on the main stage tonight.

While I know being on display isn't Knox's thing, I wanted to do this, and I know he'll do it for me. Not that he won't enjoy it. When we step out on stage, there isn't an audience, but people all over the main space can watch if they choose.

"Hey, eyes on me. No one else exists outside of you and me," Knox says.

I nod and focus on him. He leans in and places a soft kiss on my lips before his hands trail up my shoulders and then under the silk robe, which is the only thing I'm wearing. His hands lightly travel over my shoulders, pushing the silk robe slowly off my body, so it slides off and pools at my feet.

I'm on the stage completely naked, but Knox has me so focused on him it barely registers. He guides me toward the cross on the stage. When we get to it, he kisses me. Finally, he removes his lips, and his eyes lock with mine as he lifts one hand and secures it to the cross before lifting the other and doing the same.

Knox drops to his knees in front of me and spreads my legs to tie each one to its spot on the cross. His hands are gentle, but his movements are firm. After glancing at the crowd, I see that people have started to notice.

Then Knox is in front of me, and my eyes are back on him. Standing there shirtless, with his broad chest and abs on display, I swoon a little. He's only wearing sweatpants, and I know there's nothing under them. Already I can tell his big cock is hard, and he's enjoying himself. For some strange reason, that puts me even more at ease.

Stepping forward, he cups my breasts, running his thumbs over my hard nipples. His light touch tingles all the way to my core, and I want to rub my legs together, but I can't. When he pinches each nipple, I moan with pain that soon morphs into pleasure.

"What's your color, Princess?" he whispers only for my ears.

I know what he's asking. He wants to know how I'm doing being on stage, naked, tied up, and exposed to all these people. Though he doesn't want to pull us from the scene, he will if I say red.

"Green."

He nods and drops to his knees again, and let me tell you, having a strong man like Knox look up at you from his knees is intoxicating. Once I asked him about it, and he said it's the same feeling he gets when I'm on my knees giving him a blowjob. It made me understand its appeal a lot more.

Placing one hand on each of my spread thighs for balance, he leans in and goes straight for my clit. The moment his tongue makes contact, my head falls back, and I don't recognize the sound coming from me. Though that sound captures more attention because in the brief moment I look out over the crowd, more people have turned toward the stage. I look down at Knox, and he nods his head before diving back in as a reward for keeping my eyes on him.

On a mission now, he's relentless. His big hand slowly trails over my thigh as his tongue plays with my clit. All I can do is moan, hanging there helplessly. But before I realize it, he's thrusting two fingers into me and zeroes in on the spot he knows drives me crazy.

As my orgasm crashes into me, my entire body tenses and tries to collapse, but the restraints hold me up. As my orgasm recedes, I find Knox once again watching me. He kisses the inside of my thigh. Our sign for "I love you" when we're both otherwise occupied.

When he stands, he moves to the side of the cross and turns the stand so I'm no longer facing the crowd head-on but am now on a slight angle. My heart starts racing, and my body tenses up. Something that doesn't go unnoticed by Knox.

He leans in and kisses my neck, which causes me to relax instantly.

"What color, Princess?"

"Green. Just nervous."

"I've got you."

He steps back and drops his pants. He's hard and now on full display. But he only has eyes for me. If he was looking anywhere else, I don't think I'd be able to handle other women seeing him. Now I understand why he's so insistent on having my eyes on him.

He wastes no time stepping between my legs and sliding into me nice and slow, knowing it makes my body go into overdrive. We both moan, and as he slides back out, he reaches up and pinches my nipples again. The sensation makes my body turn to jello. My head falls back, and I'd collapse to the ground if the cross weren't holding me up.

Thrusting into me faster as he wraps my hair around his fist and yanks my head up. I have no choice but to look at him. The look in his eyes... it's as if he's desperate to see me, to know I'm okay. Like he needs my eyes more than I need him because this moment feels huge between us.

His lips crash into mine, and he stops all movements holding himself inside me. I whine, and he smiles.

"You feel too damn good," he whispers on my lips, dragging his cock out of me before slowly pushing back in.

Saying things like that turns me on and makes me even hotter. Having that kind of power over him is the biggest aphrodisiac. Now my sexual desire is off the charts.

He picks up his pace, and his hands dig into my hips. In the crowd, a woman screams out her orgasm. I start to turn my head to look when one of his hands grips my jaw.

"Next time, I'll have to lock your head in place. What part of 'eyes on me' do you not understand, little girl?"

Fuck.

"Sorry, Daddy," I whisper.

His eyes go from hard and angry to soft and full of love in seconds. Then he starts hammering into me. The angle has him hitting my clit each time he pounds into me, and I know he's finished playing games. He wants me to climax so he can come and drag me off the stage. What

Daddy wants, Daddy gets because a few more thrusts are all it takes for me to come harder than I ever have. The noises from the crowd enjoying our play make my orgasm even more intense.

Having his cum inside me triggers me and makes me come again. By this time, my body feels like I've run a hundred miles straight without stopping. Knox leans in and kisses me softly before pulling out of me.

With his cum trailing down my body, he drops to his knees to unhook my legs. But his eyes are on it too.

Once both my legs are free, he wraps an arm around my waist. He unhooks both arms and slips the silk robe back over me before picking me up and carrying me off the stage.

There's a small room to the side for aftercare, and he sits us on the couch with me in his lap and holds me tight. "How are you feeling, Princess?"

"I loved it. Not something I'd do every night, but I think I want to do it again. Did you like it?"

"Did I like being inside you? Making you come harder than I've ever seen? Did I like you giving me the amount of trust you did tonight? No, little girl, I fucking loved it. Every moment you give yourself to me, I crave it and want it. So, the next time you want to get up on stage, tell me. Whether it's tomorrow night or next year doesn't matter to me."

My heart races because this man knows how to drive me wild. "Take me home and make love to me." I kiss his neck, and he stands with me in his arms.

Of course, when we get home, Gemma is there to break the spell. She still has some stuff at our house and stops by to get it here and there.

"Back from the club so soon? Guess that means no sibling for me tonight," she says before shooting me a wink and heading out the door with some papers in her hand.

I can't help but laugh. That moment sums up our life, and I'm here for every second of it.

Want more of Summer and Knox? Make sure you **grab the Bonus Epilogue by signing up for my Newsletter!**

Want Skye and Gemma's stories? Get them in **Club Red: Chicago starting with Elusive Dom!**

Want Grant's story of how he ended up with his son's ex girlfriend? Get that is **Stalking His Obsession!**

Other Books by Kaci Rose

See all of Kaci Rose's Books

Oakside Military Heroes Series
Saving Noah – Lexi and Noah
Saving Easton – Easton and Paisley
Saving Teddy – Teddy and Mia
Saving Levi – Levi and Mandy
Saving Gavin – Gavin and Lauren
Saving Logan – Logan and Faith

Mountain Men of Whiskey River
Take Me To The River – Axel and Emelie
Take Me To The Cabin – Pheonix and Jenna
Take Me To The Lake – Cash and Hope

Taken By The Mountain Man

Take Me To The Mountain – Bennett and Willow

Chasing the Sun Duet

Sunrise – Kade and Lin

Sunset – Jasper and Brynn

Rock Stars of Nashville

She's Still The One – Dallas and Austin

Club Red

Daddy's Dare – Knox and Summer

Sold to my Ex's Dad

Jingling His Bells

Elusive Dom

Standalone Books

Texting Titan - Denver and Avery

Accidental Sugar Daddy – Owen and Ellie

Saving Mason - Mason and Paige

Stay With Me Now – David and Ivy

Midnight Rose - Ruby and Orlando

Committed Cowboy – Whiskey Run Cowboys
Stalking His Obsession - Dakota and Grant
Falling in Love on Route 66 - Weston and Rory
Billionaire's Marigold
Saving Ethan
Decking the Don

Connect with Kaci Rose

Website

Facebook

Kaci Rose Reader's Facebook Group

TikTok

Instagram

Twitter

Goodreads

Book Bub

Join Kaci Rose's VIP List (Newsletter)

About Kaci Rose

Kaci Rose writes steamy contemporary romance mostly set in small towns. She grew up in Florida but longs for the mountains over the beach.
She is a mom to 5 kids and a dog who is scared of his own shadow.

She also writes steamy cowboy romance as Kaci M. Rose.

Please Leave a Review!

I love to hear from my readers! Please **head over to your favorite store and leave a review** of what you thought of this book!

Made in the USA
Columbia, SC
23 September 2024